# This Coloring Book Belongs to :

___________________________

Coloring has been found to have many benefits for both adults and children. Some of the benefits of coloring include:

<u>Relaxation and stress relief</u> – Coloring can help to calm the mind and reduce stress levels. The repetitive nature of coloring can be therapeutic, helping to clear the mind and improve mental clarity.

<u>Improved focus and concentration</u> – Coloring requires concentration and focus, which can help to develop these skills and improve overall brain function.

<u>Increased creativity</u> – Coloring can help to boost creativity and imagination by allowing individuals to experiment with different colors, patterns and designs.

<u>Improved hand-eye coordination</u> – Coloring requires fine motor skills, which can help to improve hand-eye coordination and dexterity.

<u>Boosted mood and self-esteem</u> – Coloring can be a fun and engaging activity that can help to improve mood and increase feelings of self-esteem.

Overall, coloring is a simple and enjoyable activity that can bring a wide range of benefits to individuals of all ages. Whether you're looking to relieve stress, improve focus and concentration, or just have some fun, coloring is a great choice.

# Horror Beauties Coloring Book

© Copyright 2023 - All rights reserved.

A horror beauties coloring book is a fascinating and thrilling addition to the world of adult coloring books. This book is not for the faint of heart as it features a collection of spooky and unsettling illustrations that are both captivating and haunting. These drawings depict a range of beautiful but terrifying creatures that will keep you engaged and intrigued from start to finish.

Each page of this coloring book features intricate and detailed designs that allow you to bring your own personal style to the images. You can unleash your creativity and experiment with different colors to make these horror beauties come to life in your own unique way. From vampire queens to ghostly maidens, these illustrations offer a unique and macabre twist on traditional coloring books.

As you work through the pages of this coloring book, you will find yourself completely immersed in a world of horror and beauty. The striking contrast between the haunting and gorgeous aspects of these creatures creates an unnerving and thrilling coloring experience. Whether you are a horror enthusiast or simply looking for a new and exciting way to unwind, the horror beauties coloring book is sure to leave a lasting impression.

Are you ready to immerse yourself in a world of spine-tingling beauty and horror? Look no further than the horror beauties coloring book! This unique coloring experience will transport you to a realm where beauties and other eerie creatures roam free.

But don't be fooled by their striking beauty - these creatures are not to be trifled with! From a dark forest filled with ghostly maidens to a gothic castle haunted by vampire queens, this coloring book will take you on a journey through some of the most frighteningly beautiful scenes imaginable.

As you color your way through each page, you'll get to experiment with different hues and shades to bring these horror beauties to life. You'll be able to flex your artistic muscles and let your creativity run wild as you transform each drawing into a unique masterpiece.

This coloring book is not for the faint of heart, but if you're brave enough to face the horrors that await you, you're in for a treat. So grab your colored pencils and get ready to immerse yourself in a world where beauty and terror collide. The horror beauties coloring book is waiting for you!

# COLOR TEST PAGES

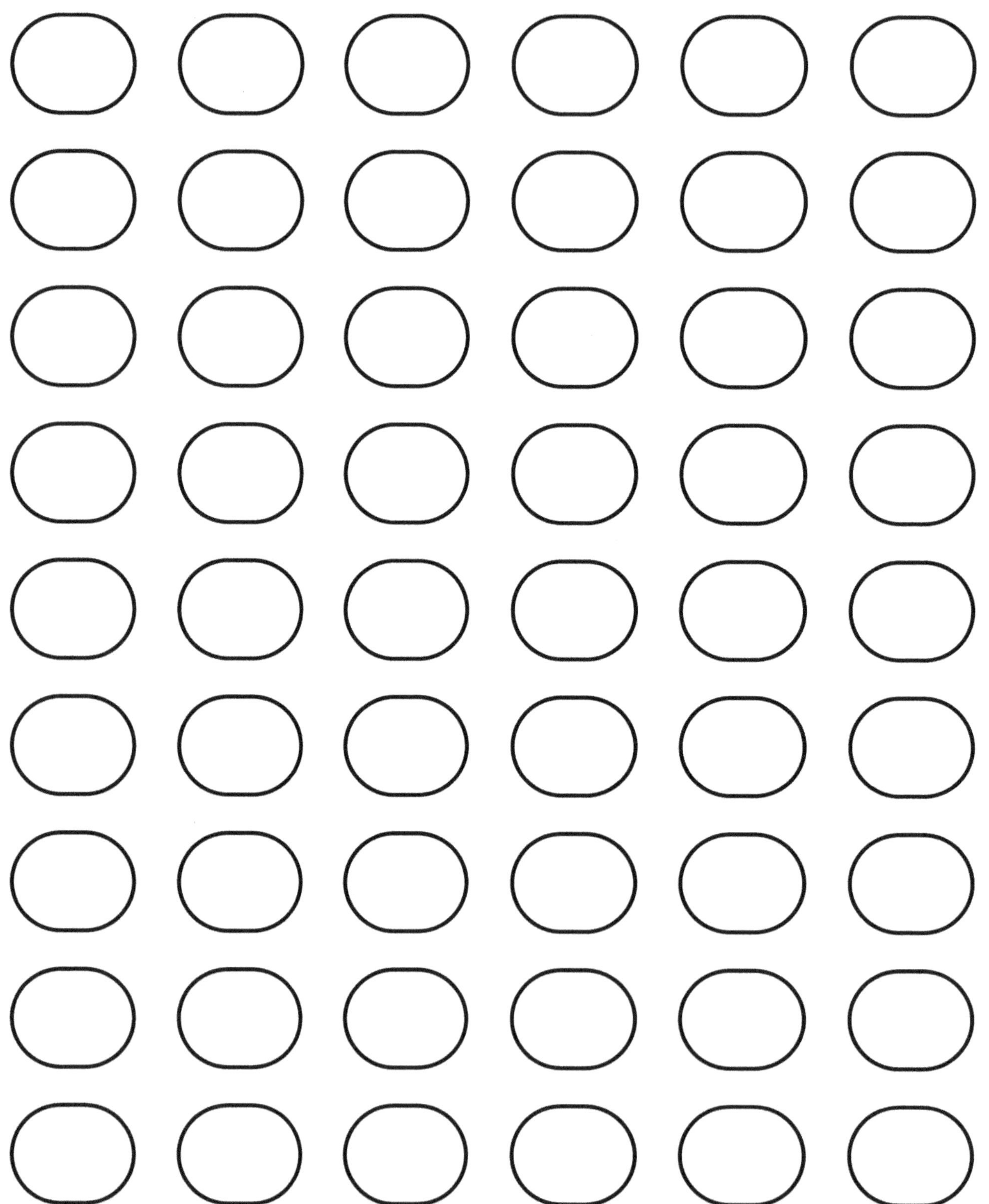

<u>We create our Books with lots of love and care !</u>

But mistakes can always happen, so if there are any issues with your book such as faulty bindings or printing errors please contact the platform you bought it to get a replacement.

**FOR QUESTIONS & SUGGESTIONS**

Email us at : lazy.black.cat.books@gmail.com

# Thank you !